Happy Punks 1 2 3
a counting story

A RULE iS To BREAK

A Child's Guide to Anarchy

by john & jana

Manic D Press
San Francisco

A Rule Is To Break ©2012 by John Seven & Jana Christy
All rights reserved. ISBN 978-1-933149-25-7
Published by Manic D Press. For information, contact
Manic D Press, PO Box 410804, San Francisco CA 94141
www.manicdpress.com
Printed in the USA by Worzalla, an employee-owned company
CPSAI compliant

The opposite of rules is

A NARChY!

There are plenty of ways to make anarchy.

Be

YOU!

When someone says, "Work!", you say

Educate yourself.

Use your

Brain.

HUG

the ugliest monster you can find!

HOLIDAY!

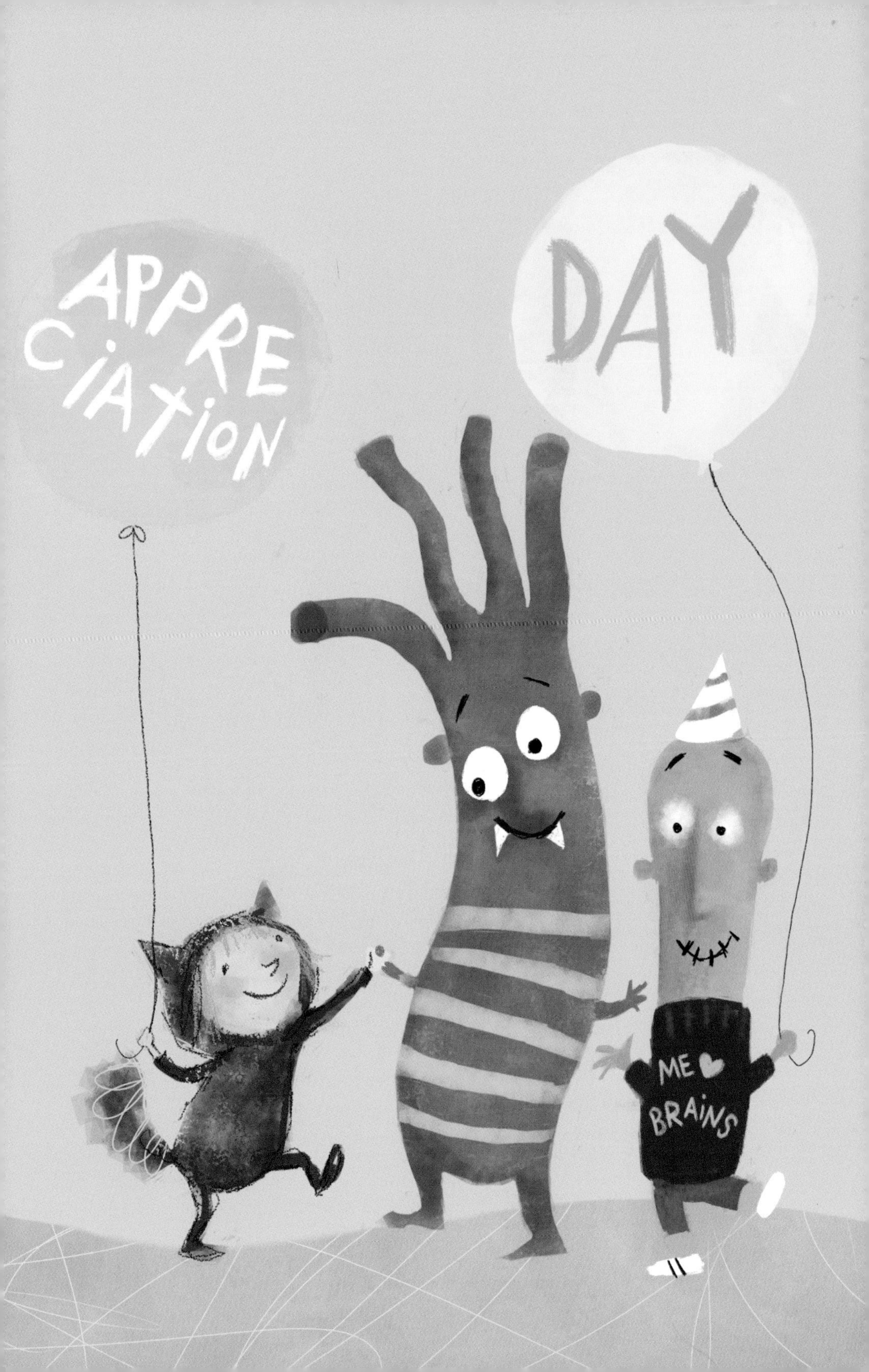
APPRECIATION
DAY
ME ♥ BRAINS

Forget about grocery stores and get

In your garden!

FREE.

CAKE!

For!

Dinner!

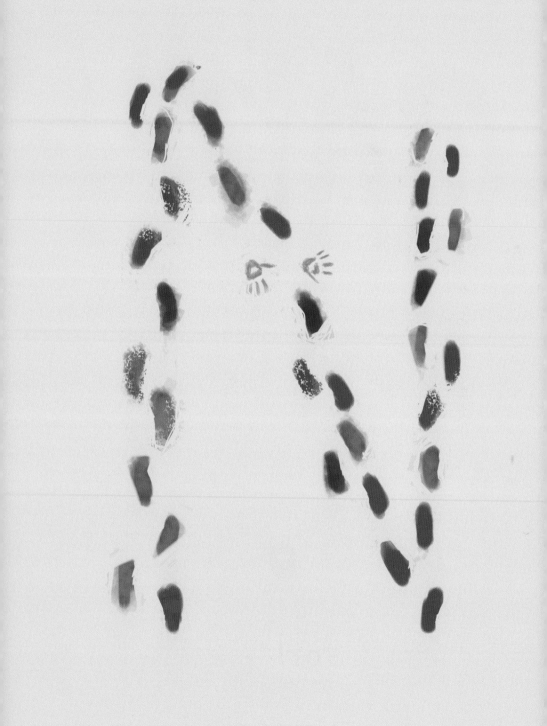

baths ever again!

SPEAK

your mind.

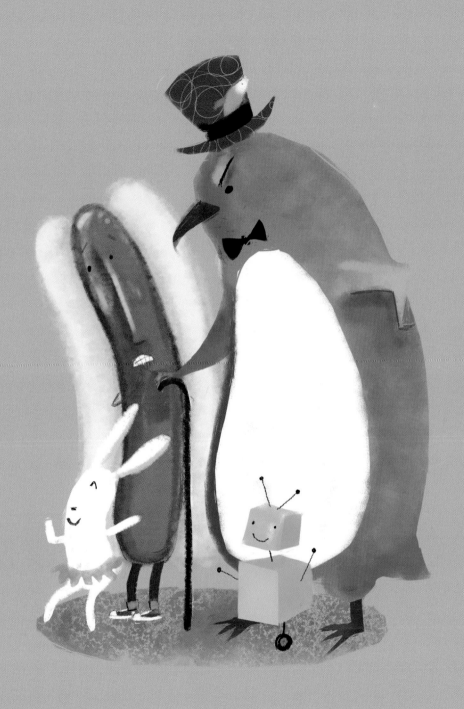

LISTEN

to the tiniest voice.

STOMPY!

BUILD IT.

Don't buy it.

Make Music

even if you don't know how.

STAY
UP

all night!

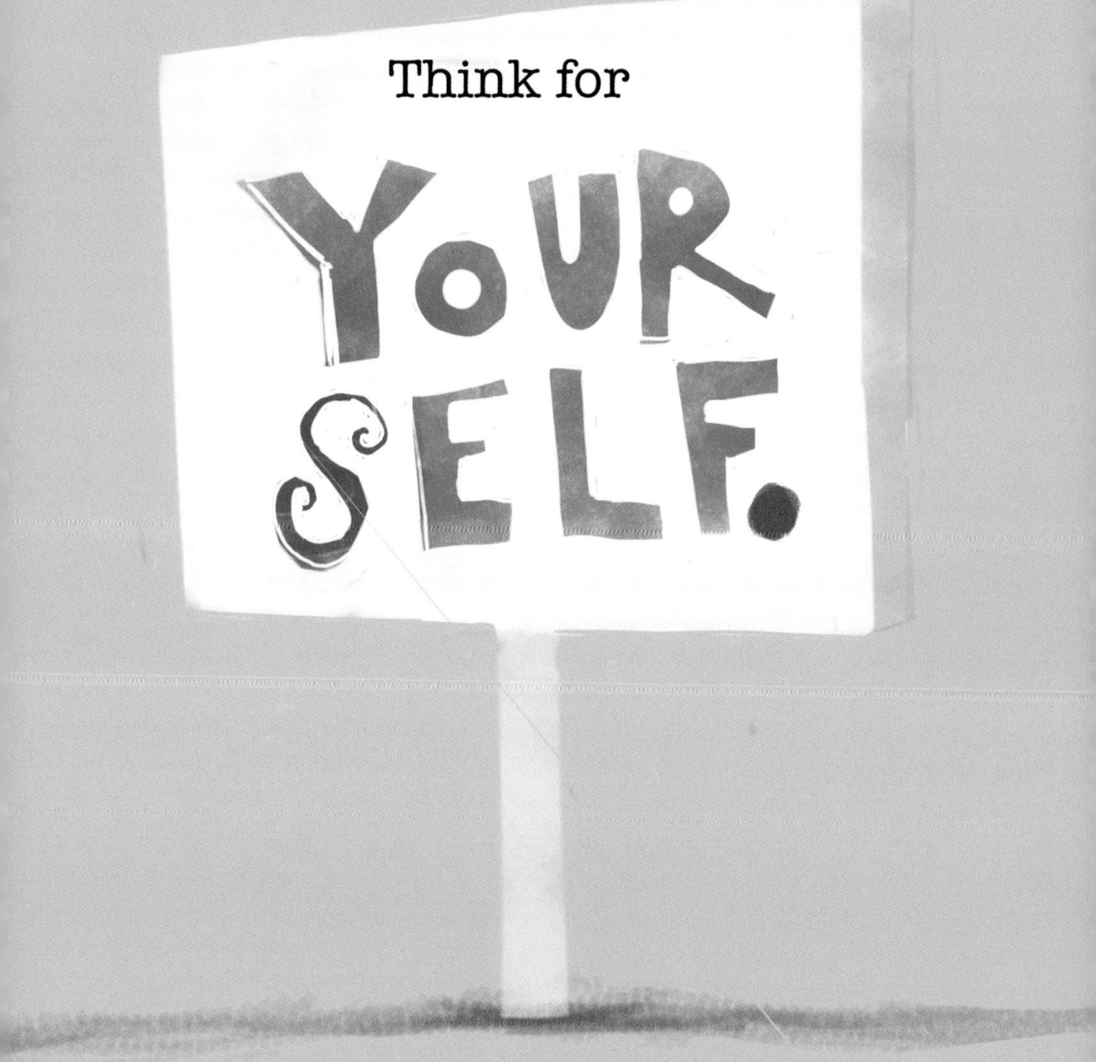
Think for
YOUR
SELF.

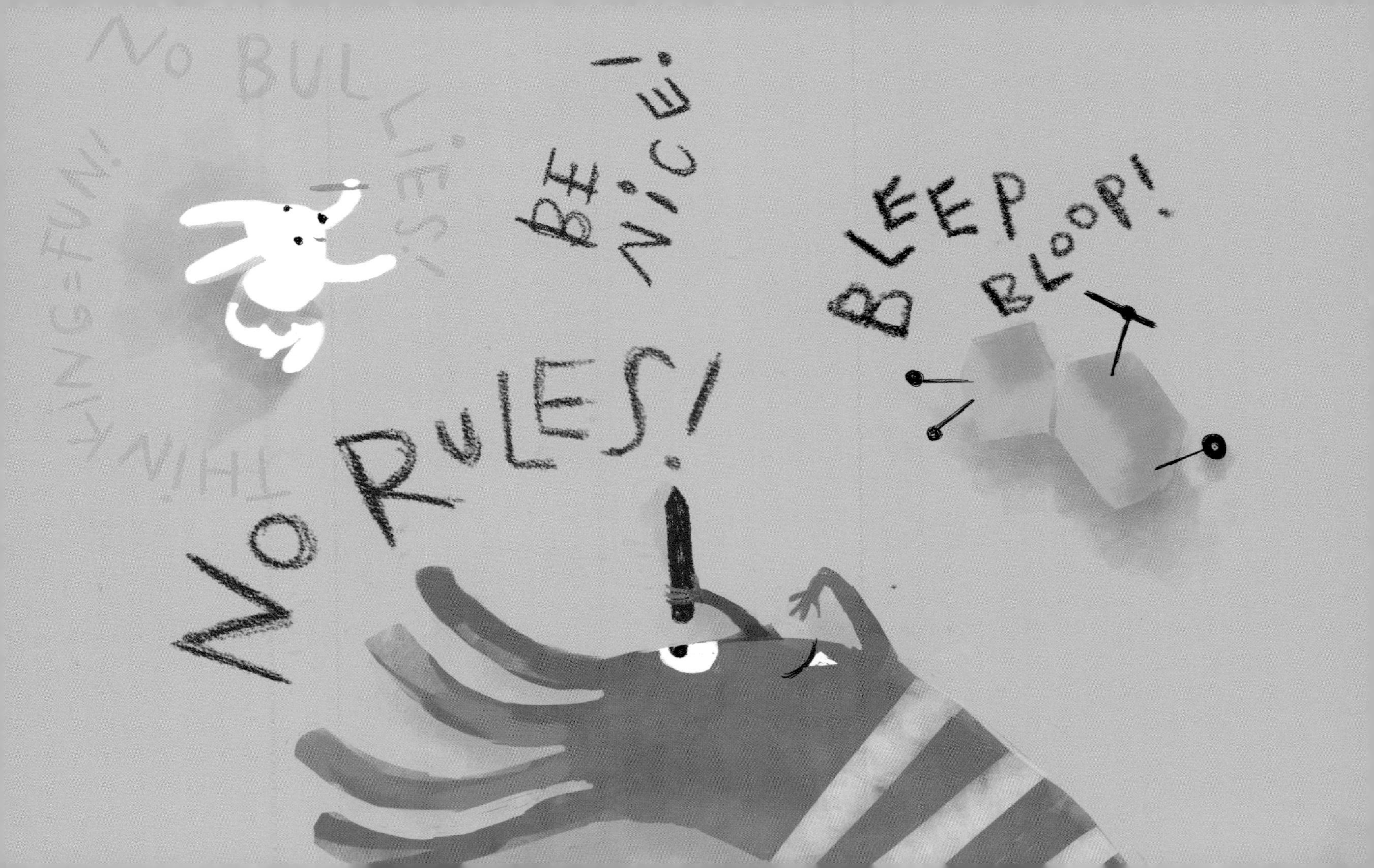
THINKING=FUN!
NO BULLIES!
NO RULES!
BE NICE!
BLEEP BLOOP!

NO KINGS!
TEAR THIS BOOK UP!
I am a VERY important CEPHALOPOD!
EAT MORE KRILL!

(or do nothing, if you prefer.)